Drip, Drop

story by Sarah Weeks
pictures by Jane Manning

HarperCollins*Publishers*

HarperCollins®, 🐾®, and I Can Read Book®
are trademarks of HarperCollins Publishers Inc.

Drip, Drop
Text copyright © 2000 by Sarah Weeks
Illustrations copyright © 2000 by Jane Manning
Manufactured in China. All rights reserved.
For information address HarperCollins Children's
Books, a division of HarperCollins Publishers,
195 Broadway, New York, NY 10007.
www.harperchildrens.com

Library of Congress Cataloging-in-Publication Data
Weeks, Sarah.
    Drip, drop / story by Sarah Weeks ; pictures by Jane Manning.
        p.   cm. — (An I can read book)
    Summary: Pip Squeak the mouse is kept awake all night by the drips from his leaky roof.
    ISBN 0-06-028523-0 — ISBN 0-06-028524-9 (lib. bdg.) — ISBN 0-06-443597-0 (pbk.)
    [1. Mice—Fiction.   2. Rain and rainfall—Fiction.   3. Stories in rhyme.]   I. Manning, Jane,
ill.   II. Title.   III. Series.
PZ8.3.W4125 Dr   2000   00-021652
[E]—dc21   CIP
                                                                                                                      AC

First Harper Trophy Edition, 2002
15 16 17 18 SCP 20
❖

For Jilly Vanilly
—*S.W.*

For Nick K., with thanks
—*J.M.*

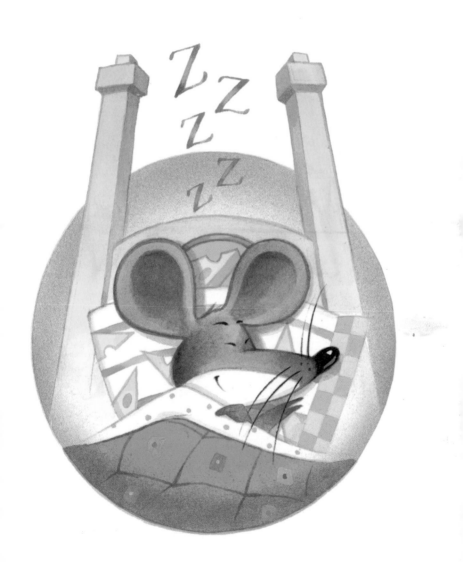

Pip Squeak lay in his bed.

Something wet fell

on his head.

Drip! Drop!

Plip! Plop!

"Oh, no!" cried Pip Squeak.

"I've got a leak!"

He climbed up

and got a cup.

6

"This cup will do the trick,"

he said.

Off he went, back to bed.

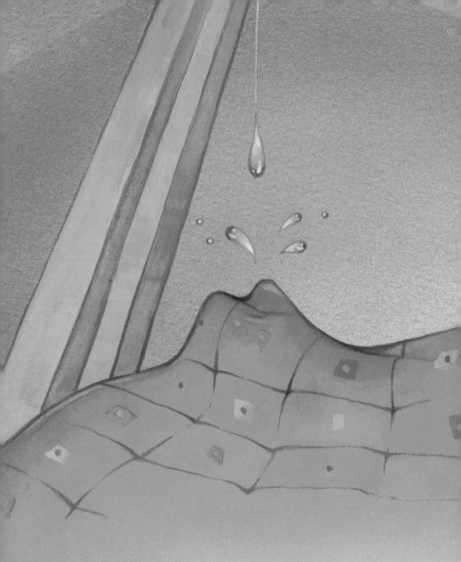

His eyes had just begun to close.

Then something wet

fell on his toes.

Drip! Drop!

Plip! Plop!

"Oh, no!" cried Pip Squeak.

"I've got a new leak."

Away he ran

to get a pan.

"This pan will do the trick,"

he said.

Off he went, back to bed.

He closed his eyes
and snuggled in.
Then something wet
fell on his chin.
Drip! Drop!
Plip! Plop!
"Oh, no!" cried Pip Squeak.
"I've got another leak."

He went and got
a great big pot.

"This pot will do the trick,"

he said.

Off he went, back to bed.

Thunder boomed!

Lightning flashed!

A new leak splished,
another splashed.

Drip! Drop!

Plip! Plop!

Down came the rain.

It would not stop.

It filled the pot.

It filled the pan.

It filled the cup.

It filled the can.

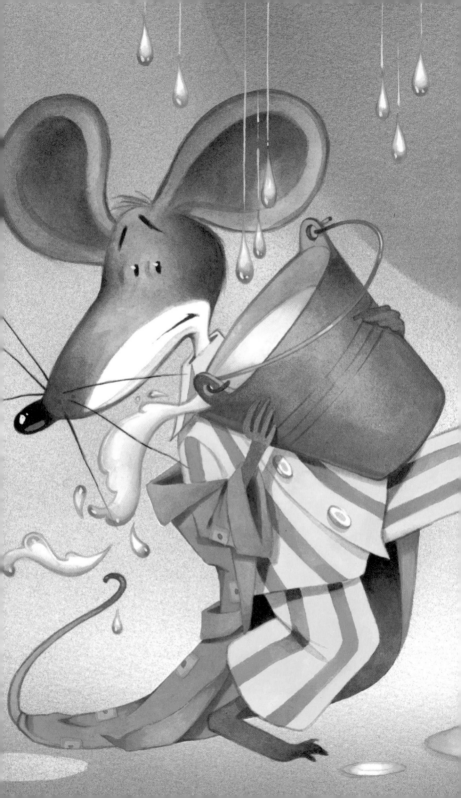

It filled the pail,

and after that

it filled the glass.

It filled the hat.

It filled the tub.

It filled the shoe.

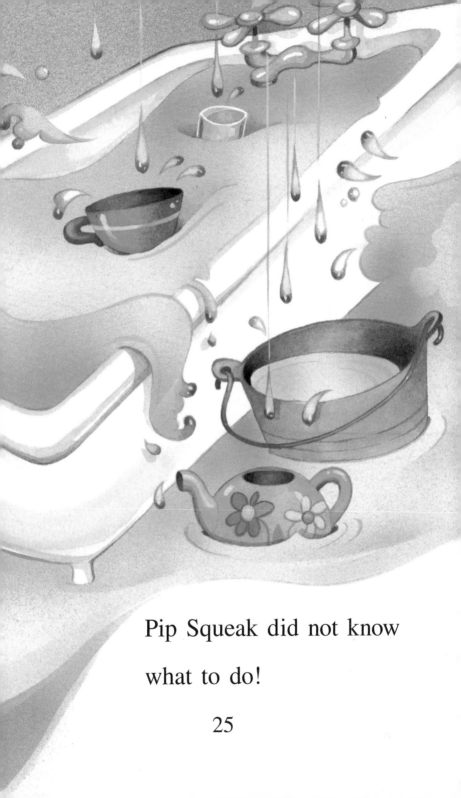

Pip Squeak did not know
what to do!

There was nothing left
to catch the drips or drops
or plips or plops.

26

"I give up," said Pip Squeak.

"Just go ahead and leak!"

He hung his head
and closed his eyes.
Then Pip Squeak
had a big surprise.

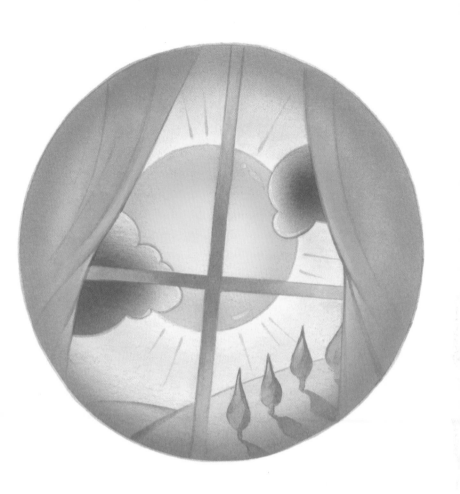

The sun came out.

The rain had stopped.

No drops dripped.

No plips plopped.

29

"Come jump in the puddles,"

his friends all said.

But Pip Squeak ran

and jumped in . . .

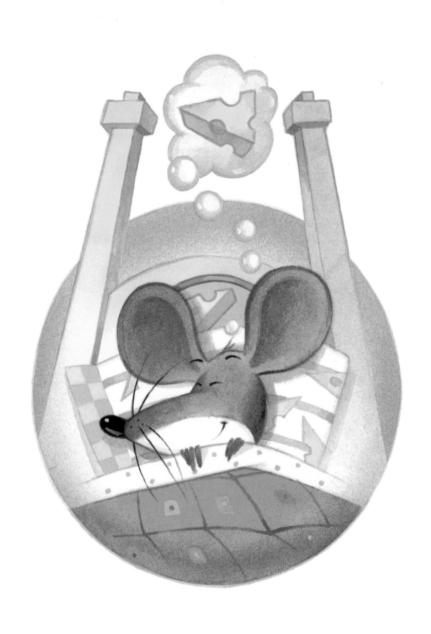

. . . bed.